Parents and Caregivers,

Stone Arch Readers are designed to provide enjoyable reading experiences, as well as opportunities to develop vocabulary, literacy skills, and comprehension. Here are a few ways to support your beginning reader:

- Talk with your child about the ideas addressed in the story.

- Discuss each illustration, mentioning the characters, where they are, and what they are doing.

- Read with expression, pointing to each word. You may want to read the whole story through and then revisit parts of the story to ensure that the meanings of words or phrases are understood.

- Talk about why the character did what he or she did and what your child would do in that situation.

- Help your child connect with characters and events in the story.

Remember, reading with your child should be fun, not forced. Each moment spent reading with your child is a priceless investment in his or her literacy life.

Gail Saunders-Smith, Ph.D.

STONE ARCH READERS

are published by Stone Arch Books
A Capstone Imprint
151 Good Counsel Drive, P.O. Box 669
Mankato, Minnesota 56002
www.capstonepub.com

Library of Congress Cataloging-in-Publication Data
　　Meister, Cari.
　　The hiding eel / by Cari Meister; illustrated by Steve Harpster.
　　p. cm. — (Stone Arch readers. Ocean tales)
　　Summary: Leon the eel hides from Fifi the grouper fish until he must come out
for food.
　　ISBN 978-1-4342-3199-4 (library binding)
　　ISBN 978-1-4342-3390-5 (pbk.)
　　[1. Eels—Fiction. 2. Fishes—Fiction. 3. Hide-and-seek—Fiction.] I. Harpster,
Steve, ill. II. Title.
PZ7.M515916Hi 2011
[E]—dc22

2011000299

Art Director: Kay Fraser
Designer: Emily Harris
Production Specialist: Michelle Biedscheid

Reading Consultants:

Gail Saunders-Smith, Ph.D.
Melinda Melton Crow, M.Ed.
Laurie K. Holland, Media Specialist

Printed in the United States of America in Melrose Park, Illinois.
032011
006112LKF11

THE Hiding EEL

by Cari Meister

illustrated by Steve Harpster

STONE ARCH BOOKS
a capstone imprint

LEON THE MORAY EEL

MORAY EEL FUN FACTS

- A moray eel looks like a snake, but it is actually a fish.

- There are more than 100 species of moray eels.

- Moray eels have a good sense of smell but a terrible sense of sight.

- A moray eel can tie itself in knots.

Leon was good at hide-and-seek.

In fact, he was the best in the reef.

One time, Leon hid for two weeks. He wanted to make sure he won.

He did. All the other fish got hungry. They left to look for food.

Leon was a spotted moray eel. He could go a long time without eating.

But things were changing
in the water. Everyone was
busy. No one wanted to play
hide-and-seek anymore.

A new fish moved in. She called herself Fifi.

"I'm a grouper fish," Fifi
told everyone. "See my pretty
spots?"

When Fifi moved to the reef,
Leon hid in his house.

"Groupers sometimes eat
eels," said Leon. "I do not want
to be Fifi's next meal."

Leon hid for three weeks.

One day, Leon heard someone knocking at his door. It was Fifi!

"Hello!" she said. "What's your name?"

Leon quickly pulled his head back in. Fifi tried to squeeze through the door, but she did not fit.

Leon hid for two more weeks.
By this time, he was very
hungry.

"I cannot wait any longer,"
he said.

Leon poked his head through the door.

Fifi was waiting. "There you are!" she said. "Are you going to hide forever?"

"Are you going to eat me?" asked Leon.

Fifi laughed. "Eat you?" she
asked. "No. I do not like eating
eel. Besides, you are too big. Let
me see the rest of you."

Leon slid all the way out.

"Look at you! What a nice fish! Great spots. Sharp teeth. Cool fins!" Fifi said.

Leon smiled. "Thank you,"
he said.

"I think you will work out just fine," Fifi said.

"I will?" asked Leon. "For what?"

"I need a hunting partner," Fifi said.

Leon did not know what to think. He always hunted alone.

"Where I come from," said Fifi, "eels and groupers hunt together all the time. We get more food that way."

"I guess it doesn't hurt to try," said Leon.

So Leon and Fifi went off hunting. Together, they caught a lot of food!

They had the best feast ever!

"We make a great team,"
said Fifi.

Leon smiled.

"Fifi," he asked, "are you any good at hide-and-seek?"

The End

STORY WORDS

hide-and-seek   squeeze

reef   forever

moray   partner

grouper

Total Word Count: 363

WHO ELSE IS SWIMMING IN THE OCEAN?